CHRISTMAS
DAY
IN THE
MORNING

CHRISTMAS
DAY
IN THE
MORNING

AWAKENING THE JOY
OF CHRISTMAS

PEARL S. BUCK

NEWLY ADAPTED BY
DAVID T. WARNER

FOR THE 2019 CHRISTMAS CONCERT OF
THE TABERNACLE CHOIR AT TEMPLE SQUARE

SHADOW
MOUNTAIN

THE
TABERNACLE
CHOIR AT TEMPLE SQUARE

Interior image credits: Page v, B.G. Photography/Shutterstock; page vi, ju_see/Shutterstock; page 2, FrameAngel/Shutterstock; page 4, Lysenko Andrii/Shutterstock; page 7, Leonsbox/iStock; page 8, tie in box The Travel Gentleman/Shutterstock, pattern by mattjeacock/iStock; page 9, Jean Valjeann/Shutterstock; page 10, B.G. Photography/Shutterstock; page 11, 00one/iStock; page 12, ananaline/Shutterstock; page 13, Jason Sponseller/Shutterstock; page 14, P2KinArt/Shutterstock; page 15, Wirestock Images/Shutterstock; page 17, Bernard Tuck/Unsplash; page 18–19, barn by Jason Sponseller/Shutterstock, sky by Vitalii Bashkatov/Shutterstock, star by RealCG Animation Studio/Shutterstock; page 20, Suzanne Tucker/Shutterstock; page 22, K N/Shutterstock; page 23, VLADIMIR DUDKIN/Shutterstock; page 24, Inkout/iStock; page 25, children holding doll and gift by SuperStock Alamy Stock Photo, children with drums by ClassicStock/Alamy Stock Photo, mother stacking gifts by ClassicStock/Alamy Stock Photo; page 26, New Africa/Shutterstock; page 27, Roman Safonov/Shutterstock; page 29, Rawpixel.com/shutterstock; page 31, BrianSM/istock; page 32, Elenadesign/Shutterstock; page 38, Liptak Robert/Shutterstock; page 42, B.G. Photography/Shutterstock.

The Tabernacle Choir and Orchestra at Temple Square provide artistic expressions of faith from The Church of Jesus Christ of Latter-day Saints.

Visit us at ShadowMountain.com

Library of Congress Cataloging-in-Publication Data

Names: Warner, David T. (David Terry), 1963– author. | Buck, Pearl S. (Pearl Sydenstricker), 1892–1973. Christmas day in the morning. | The Tabernacle Choir at Temple Square.
Title: Christmas Day in the morning : awakening the joy of Christmas / Pearl S. Buck ; newly adapted by David T. Warner for the 2019 Christmas concert of The Tabernacle Choir at Temple Square.
Description: Salt Lake City : Shadow Mountain : The Tabernacle Choir at Temple Square, [2020] | "Lyrics within this story come from a song performed by The Tabernacle Choir and Orchestra at Temple Square as part of their 2019 Christmas concert." | Summary: "An adaptation of Pearl S. Buck's classic Christmas story, this text was used as part of The Tabernacle Choir at Temple Square's annual Christmas concert in 2019"—Provided by publisher.
Identifiers: LCCN 2020017522 | ISBN 9781629727967 (hardback)
Subjects: LCSH: Farm life—Fiction. | LCGFT: Christmas fiction. | Short stories.
Classification: LCC PS3623.A86255 C49 2020 | DDC 813/.6—dc23
LC record available at https://lccn.loc.gov/2020017522

Printed in China
RR Donnelley, Dongguan, China

10   9   8   7   6   5   4   3   2   1

Lyrics within this story come from

an American folk hymn performed by

The Tabernacle Choir and Orchestra

at Temple Square as part of their

2019 Christmas concert.

———— ✴ ————

Robert woke suddenly and completely. It was four o'clock, the hour when his father had always called him to get up and help with the milking. That was fifty years ago, but his eyes still opened every morning at four. And even if he wanted to go back to sleep—which he usually did— it wasn't going to happen this morning, because this morning was Christmas.

He looked at his wife sleeping beside him and remembered Christmases when their children were young. This had been a joyous day—the day she labored and lived for, filled with the laughter of little ones. But now those children were grown and the house was empty, and for her Christmas was becoming just another winter morning, its joy a memory

of the past. His mind slipped back further,

to growing up on his father's farm. He had

always loved his father, but he hadn't realized

how much. And then one day he overheard his

parents talking.

I wish I didn't have to get Robby up so early," his father said. "He's growin' so fast, and he needs his sleep. If I could just find a way to handle the milkin' alone . . . ."

"Well, you can't," his mother said firmly. "Besides, he's not a child anymore, and it's time he do his part."

"It's true," said his father. "But I still don't like to wake him."

———— ✳ ————

Hearing those words, something awakened in Rob. His father loved him! He had never thought of it before, but now he knew it. And he could never go back to waiting for his father to call him in the mornings, again and again. He might stumble out of bed blind with sleep, pulling on his clothes with his eyes half shut. But he would get up.

A few days later, on Christmas Eve, Rob was lying in his bed thinking about the next morning. His family was poor, and most of their excitement was about the turkey they raised themselves and mince pies his mother made.

His parents always gave him something he needed, and he saved to buy them gifts, too. For his father, it was always a tie from the ten-cent store. But that Christmas, the tie just wasn't enough. Rob had to give him something better—something more.

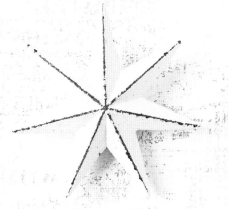

R ob lay on his side, propped up on one elbow, looking out the attic window. The stars were bright, much brighter than he ever remembered them. And he wondered if one of them was the star that shone over Bethlehem.

O watch the stars,
see how they run.

O watch the stars,
see how they run.

The stars run down
at the setting of the sun.

O watch the stars,
see how they run.

D ad," Rob once asked when he was a little boy, "What's a stable?"

"It's just a barn," his father had replied, "like ours."

So, Jesus had been born in a barn! And to a barn the shepherds had come, and Wise Men with their gifts. In that moment, a thought struck Rob like lightning: They had a barn, and in it there was a gift for him to give. He would get up before four o'clock and milk the cows. He'd do it alone, while everyone was asleep, and when his father opened the barn door, all the work would be done. A smile broke across Rob's face and his eyes danced with the stars.

Go find the Child,

see where He lies.

Go find the Child,

see where He lies.

He sweetly lies

wrapped in Mary's lullabies.

Go find the Child,

see where He lies.

R ob must have woken twenty times that night, scratching a match each time to look at his old watch. Midnight. One o'clock. Half past two. At a quarter to three he finally got up and put on his clothes, crept downstairs (being careful of the creaky boards), and let himself out.

I nside the barn, he lit the old hurricane lamp. The cows were looking at him, sleepy and surprised. It was early for them, too. Then, with a great rush of energy Rob set to work. He smiled as he milked steadily, two strong streams rushing into the pail, frothing and fragrant. For once, milking was not a chore. It was something else—a gift to his father who loved him.

When he finished, the two milk cans were perfectly full. He covered them and closed the milk house door carefully, making sure of the latch.

Back in his room he had only a minute to pull off his clothes in the darkness and jump into bed. His father was already coming down the hall. Rob yanked the covers over his head as the door opened.

R ob! We have to get up, son . . ."

"Aw-right," he mumbled.

The door closed and Rob lay still, breathing heavily. In just a few minutes his father would know. His heart was ready to jump from his body.

The minutes seemed endless—ten, fifteen, he didn't know how many—until he heard his father's footsteps. Again, the door opened.

R obert!"

"Yes, Dad—"

His father was laughing, a strange sobbing sort of laugh. "Thought you'd fool me, did you?" His father was standing by his bed, feeling for him, pulling away the covers.

"It's for Christmas!" Rob cried, finding his father and clutching him in a great hug. He felt his father's arms around him in the dark.

"Son, I thank you. Nobody ever did a nicer thing—"

"Oh, Dad," Rob said, "I just want to be good!" The words broke from him of their own will. His heart was bursting with joy.

Fifty years later, Robert reflected on that Christmas, and again something in him awakened. He looked over at his wife and remembered the years of Christmas mornings she had made joyous for him and their children. In that moment, all he wanted was to give her something, to do something to express his love and revive their joy.

A nd then it struck him like lightning:
The true joy of Christmas is to love and
to awaken love. Their children were grown
and their house was empty, and the laughter
of little ones would remain a memory. And
yet, because of his father's love, and because
of hers, love was alive in him. And the joy of
Christmas was his to give.

———— ✳ ————

Quietly, he got up in the dark, pulled on his clothes as he had done so many years before, and crept to his desk (being careful of the creaky boards). "My dearest love," he wrote, his pen flowing freely across milk-white paper.

On this Christmas day, on this
Christmas day in the morning . . .
Merry Christmas, my love.
Your husband, Rob.

Behold the Lamb,

see how He loves.

Behold the Lamb,

see how He loves.

The Lamb loves you,

and will bring you

home above.

O watch the stars . . .

Go find the Child . . .

Behold the Lamb,

see how He loves!

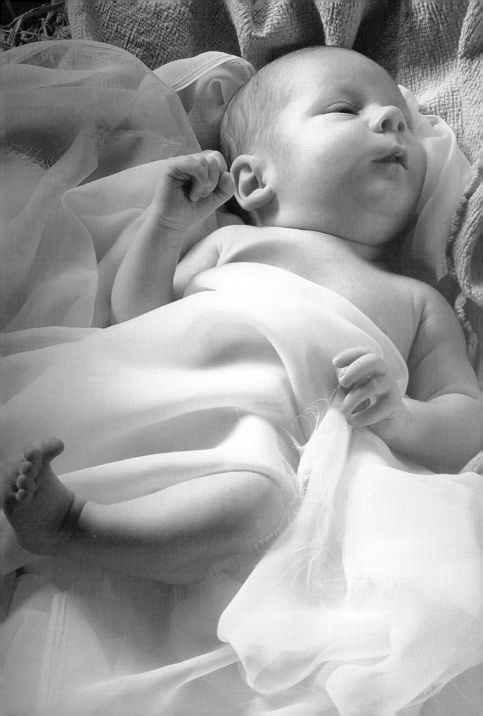

A LETTER OF GRATITUDE AND LOVE

O watch the stars, see how they run.

O watch the stars, see how they run.

The stars run down at the setting of the sun.

O watch the stars, see how they run.

Go find the Child, see where He lies.

Go find the Child, see where He lies.

He sweetly lies wrapped in Mary's lullabies.

Go find the Child, see where He lies.

Behold the Lamb, see how He loves.

Behold the Lamb, see how He loves.

The Lamb loves you, and will bring you home above.

O watch the stars . . . Go find the Child . . .

Behold the Lamb, see how He loves!

---- ✳ ----

PEARL SYDENSTRICKER BUCK was born in 1892 in Hillsboro, West Virginia, to parents who were Christian missionaries. She grew up primarily in Zhenjiang, China, spending most of her life there from the time she was five months old until her early forties. She was raised speaking both English and Chinese and considered herself American by birth and ancestry but shaped by Chinese culture in how she wrote and told stories.

In addition to teaching university-level English literature courses, Buck was a prolific writer of novels, short stories, children's books, and nonfiction. She published over seventy books in a career spanning four decades, and she was widely recognized as a voice bridging the East and the West. She first made her mark in the literary world with the publication of her novel *The Good Earth*, which was a best seller and won the Pulitzer Prize in 1932. In 1938, Buck became the first American woman to win the Nobel Prize for Literature "for her rich and truly epic descriptions of peasant life in China and for her biographical masterpieces."

In her later years, Buck devoted much of her time to humanitarian efforts. Through her writing, she spread awareness about issues that were important to her, including racism, sexism, immigration, missionary work, war, refugees, and violence. She was known for being an advocate for women and a champion of minority rights, particularly invested in making adoption services available for Asian and mixed-race children.

In 1955, Buck published "Christmas Day in the Morning" in *Collier's* magazine.

Every December, one of the many wonders of Christmas in Salt Lake City is the annual concert of The Tabernacle Choir and Orchestra at Temple Square, a Temple Square tradition for decades. Since 2000, these popular concerts have delighted live audiences of over 60,000 people each year in the Conference Center of The Church of Jesus Christ of Latter-day Saints, with millions more tuning in to *Christmas with The Tabernacle Choir* on PBS through the partnership of WGBH and BYU Television. It is a full-scale production featuring world-class musicians, soloists, dancers, narrators, and music that delights viewers each year.

Each concert has featured a special guest artist, including Broadway actors and singers Kelli O'Hara (2019), Kristin Chenoweth (2018), Sutton Foster (2017), Laura Osnes (2015), Santino Fontana (2014), Alfie Boe (2012), and Brian Stokes Mitchell (2011); opera stars Rolando Villazón (2016), Deborah Voigt (2013), Nathan Gunn (2011), Renée Fleming (2005),

Bryn Terfel (2003) and Frederica von Stade (2003); Grammy Award–winner Natalie Cole (2009), *American Idol* finalist David Archuleta (2010); and the Muppets® from Sesame Street® (2014). The remarkable talents of award-winning actors Richard Thomas (2019), Hugh Bonneville (2017), Martin Jarvis (2015), John Rhys-Davies (2013), Jane Seymour (2011), Michael York (2010), and Edward Herrmann (2008) have graced the stage, sharing memorable stories of the season. Featured narrators also include famed broadcast journalist Tom Brokaw (2012), two-time Pulitzer Prize–winning author David McCullough (2009), and noted TV news anchorman Walter Cronkite (2002).

The 360 members of the The Tabernacle Choir represent men and women from many different backgrounds and professions and range in age from twenty-five to sixty. Their companion ensemble, the Orchestra at Temple Square, includes a roster of more than 200 musicians who accompany the Choir on broadcasts, recordings, and tours. All serve as unpaid volunteers with a mission of sharing inspired music that has the power to bring people closer to the divine.

The Tabernacle Choir has appeared at thirteen world's fairs and expositions, performed at the inaugurations of seven U.S. presidents, and sung for numerous worldwide telecasts and special events. Five of The Tabernacle Choir's recordings have achieved "gold record" and two have achieved "platinum record" status. Its recordings have reached the #1 position on *Billboard*® magazine's classical lists a remarkable thirteen times since 2003.

This adaptation of the Pearl S. Buck's "Christmas Day in the Morning" was originally made for the 2019 Christmas concert, narrated by Richard Thomas, with music by the Choir and Orchestra. You can enjoy that performance at www.TabChoir.org/ChristmasDayintheMorning.